Off to Elephant School

by James Preller

SCHOLASTIC INC.

New York   Toronto   London   Auckland   Sydney

Exclusive worldwide licensing agent: Momentum Partners, Inc., New York, NY
Photo credits:
All graphic maps: Lisa Kelly
Cover: All photos Anthony Bannister/ © 1996 Paragon Entertainment Corporation.
Interior: **pp. 2, 3** Anthony Bannister/ ©1996 Paragon Entertainment Corporation; **p. 4** (top) Photo by Anthony Bannister/ © 1996 Paragon Entertainment Corporation; (bottom) © Leonard Lee Rue III; **p. 5** Anthony Bannister/ © 1996 Paragon Entertainment Corporation; **pp. 6-7** © Johnny Johnson/DRK Photo; **p. 8** All photos © 1996 Paragon Entertainment Corporation; **p. 9** (left) © Art Wolfe/Tony Stone Images; (center) © Gerry Ellis Nature Photography; (right) © M.P. Kahl/Photo Researchers; **p. 10** All photos by Anthony Bannister/ © 1996 Paragon Entertainment Corporation; **p. 11** (left) © Fritz Polking/Peter Arnold, Inc.; (right) © Kevin Schafer/Peter Arnold, Inc.; **p. 12** Anthony Bannister/ © 1996 Paragon Entertainment Corporation; **p. 13** All photos by Anthony Bannister/ © 1996 Paragon Entertainment Corporation; **p. 14** (top) Anthony Bannister/ © 1996 Paragon Entertainment Corporation; (bottom) © 1996 Paragon Entertainment Corporation; **p. 15** © M. P. Kahl/DRK Photo; **p. 16** Chris Harvey/ © Tony Stone Worldwide; **p. 17** (top) © Leonard Lee Rue III; (bottom) Anthony Bannister/ © 1996 Paragon Entertainment Corporation; **pp. 18-19** Anthony Bannister/ © 1996 Paragon Entertainment Corporation; **p. 20** © Leonard Lee Rue III; **pp. 21-24** All photos Anthony Bannister/ © 1996 Paragon Entertainment Corporation; **p. 25** © Gerry Ellis Nature Photography; **pp. 26-27** © Leonard Lee Rue III; **p. 28** © Martin Harvey/The Wildlife Collection; (insert) © 1996 Paragon Entertainment Corporation; **p. 29** © Leonard Lee Rue III; **pp. 30-31** © 1996 Paragon Entertainment Corporation; **p. 32** Anthony Bannister/ © 1996 Paragon Entertainment Corporation.

ISBN 0-590-53740-7

Book design by Todd Lefelt

12 11 10 9 8 7 6 5 4 3 2 1   6 7 8 9/9 0 1/0

Printed in the U.S.A.   23

First Scholastic printing, October 1996

What is the largest land animal in the world?

A rhinoceros?

Good guess, but not quite.

A hippopotamus?

You're getting close.

A giraffe?

That's the tallest. But not the largest. Okay, we'll give you a clue. **It's got really big ears!**

The answer is...

an
elephant!

Some of the biggest elephants weigh more than seven tons!

FunFact #1

African elephants stand 10–12 feet tall and can weigh as much as 16,500 pounds. They live on flat, grassy areas called savannas. Asian elephants live in rain forests and normally do not weigh more than 10,000 pounds. Smaller, yes. But you still wouldn't want to let one sit on your bicycle!

African Elephant

Asian Elephant

African Elephant

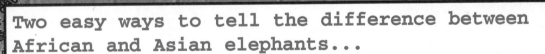

Two easy ways to tell the difference between African and Asian elephants...

1. An African elephant's ears are more than twice as large as those of an Asian elephant. An Asian elephant has ears that are more triangular in shape than those of an African elephant.

2. An African elephant's trunk has two fingerlike knobs that allow him to hold on to things. An Asian elephant has only one knob on his trunk.

Kenya

Here we are at the Sheldrick Wildlife Trust in Kenya, East Africa. It's a special home for elephants that have been orphaned in the wild.

We're here to hang out with Emily, a two-year-old elephant. Emily would be all alone if it weren't for the wonderful people here at Sheldrick.

Baby elephants need protection from dangerous predators such as lions, hyenas, and crocodiles. Luckily, the elder elephants in the herd protect the younger ones. The grown-up elephants have only one predator to fear...humans!

Hyena

Lion

The Sad Truth

Some humans illegally kill elephants for their ivory tusks. These hunters are known as poachers. The poachers sell the ivory for a lot of money. Each year, poachers shoot thousands of elephants. This leaves many baby elephants without mothers to teach them how to survive in the wild.

Before she can live among an elephant herd, Emily will have to learn how to survive in the wild. Normally, her mother would have taught her all she needed to know. But because Emily's an orphan, the workers at the Sheldrick Wildlife Trust will be her teachers.

Emily will be about 12 years old when she is ready to join a herd. Until then, the people at Sheldrick will be her family, giving her everything she needs to help her grow healthy and strong—including a sense of security and lots of love.

When orphaned elephants first come to Sheldrick they are often sad and depressed. They miss their elephant families. Caretakers need to spend every minute with Emily—even sleeping with her.

Taking care of an elephant isn't as easy as taking care of a pet hamster or goldfish. For starters, Emily needs food. Lots of it!

Baby Elephant Menu

Milk

Grass

Leaves

Tree bark

Roots

Dirt

Hey! What do you feed a 600-pound elephant?

Anything she wants, Martin!

That was just a joke. But it is important that Emily get a healthy diet.

Baby elephants in the wild suckle for two years. But at three months, they begin to eat some vegetation—pretty much whatever is available. A grown elephant could easily eat more than 350 pounds of food a day!

FunFact #2

Elephants eat all the time. All that chewing, grinding, and mashing can wear down their teeth. Luckily, as one set of teeth gets worn down, another grows in its place. Elephants can grow six sets of teeth during a lifetime.

This is a photo of an adult elephant's molar. It can weigh as much as ten pounds!

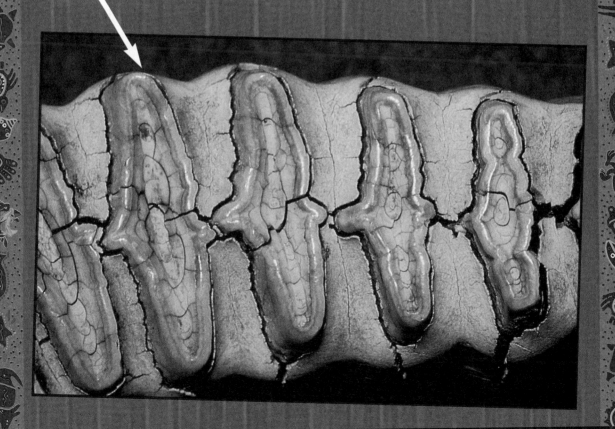

Creature Feature
A Salute to the Fabulous, Incredible, Splendiferous Trunk!

Who wouldn't want a trunk? It would be like having an arm and a hand...stuck to the end of your nose! An elephant's trunk is actually part nose and part upper lip, joined together.

Here are some of the ways elephant trunks come in handy:

● **Trunks can get into those hard-to-reach places.**

They are powerful.

And sensitive.

Elephants just want to have fun!

But in Emily's case, play is more than just fun. Playing games like soccer gives Emily a chance to use her muscles and her brain. Elephants are herd animals. They need to be with, and learn from, others.

Hey, good kick, Emily!

FunFact #3

Elephants drink up to 40 gallons of water a day. You'd have to drink a 170-foot tall glass of water to drink what an elephant does! Talk about needing a big straw!

It is important for Emily to grow up in an environment as close to her natural one as possible. And one thing that's natural for Emily is...

...taking wonderful, cool, messy **mud baths!**

Mud baths sure are more fun than plain old soap and water!

23

Actually, mud baths are very important for elephants. The mud and water get trapped deep down in the wrinkles of Emily's skin. That helps keep Emily cool and protects her from the rays of the hot African sun. Mud baths are the elephant version of suntan lotion!

Elephants really love their mud baths. But if there isn't any water around, elephants will take dust baths. They vacuum dust into their trunks, and then blow it all over themselves. The dust helps protect their skin from insects and sunburn.

Creature Feature
A Closer Look at Nature's Magnificent Design!

An elephant's body is an amazing work of nature. Powerful tusks, flexible trunk, wrinkly skin, big ears – each body part has an important job to do. Here's a closer look:

Tusks

Tusks are basically teeth that keep growing ... and growing ... and growing! Some tusks weigh as much as 130 pounds. Tusks are strong, too. They can pry apart tree branches, strip bark from trees, and even drill holes for water or salt.

Ears

An elephant uses his ears for hearing – of course. But those giant ears are also used to scare off possible enemies. They also serve as portable cooling fans, helping to release body heat.

Feet

An elephant's foot is perfectly designed to carry his enormous weight. His feet are large and round. They have a pad of fat on the sole. This design distributes the elephant's weight over a large area. That makes walking a lot more comfortable! In fact, that fatty pad can make the elephant feel like he is walking on pillows. Most times, elephants don't even leave footprints – which is not an easy trick for an animal that weighs more than five tons!

When Emily returns to the savanna, she'll have to be accepted into a wild herd. The herd will become her new family.

But I think she'll always remember the good people who cared for her.

The herd is a group of female elephants, plus their babies of both sexes. Once the male elephants grow up, they go off to live on their own.

The leader of the herd is called the *matriarch*. She's usually the biggest and oldest female.

Elephant moms are caring, gentle, and protective. All the females in the herd lend a hand (or a trunk) in raising the babies.

FUN Fact #4

In the wild, baby elephants often stand underneath their mothers. This protects them from rain, sun, and wind. It's sort of like having a 12,000-pound umbrella!

THE *END*!